Here in Space

Written and Illustrated
by David Milgrim

BridgeWater Paperback

*This book is dedicated
to everyone who wonders.*

First published in hardcover by BridgeWater Books.

First paperback edition published 1998.

Printed in the United States of America.

10   9   8   7   6   5   4   3   2   1

Library of Congress Cataloging-in-Publication Data

Milgrim, David.
Here in space / written and illustrated by David Milgrim.
p.   cm.
Summary: An imaginative young "space explorer" describes
the many fascinating features of his home on the planet Earth.
ISBN 0-8167-4393-2 (lib. bdg.) ISBN 0-8167-4462-9 (pbk.)
[1. Earth—Fiction. 2. Stories in rhyme.] I. Title.
PZ8.3.M5776He   1997
[E]—dc21   97-11373

I live in space. I have lived here since birth,

On a big ball of rock that
is called planet Earth!

Since I live on the earth, I am living in space.

And space is a strange and mysterious place.

Out here in space there's a lot to explore.

There's fire that flames from
the earth's inner core.

There are oceans so cold that they freeze into land

And many strange
creatures I
don't understand.

In space there are powerful, thundering waves

And dark, eerie silences
deep in the caves.

And questions whose answers
can never be known.

The earth is a wild, exciting frontier.

And I am a rambling space pioneer.

And here on the earth, in this magical place,

I am always at home
in the wonder of space.